Hello Kitty®

Hello Shapes!

illustrated by Higashi Glaser

ABRADALE, NEW YORK

One rainy day, Hello Kitty is playing with her toys—a ball that's round, a block that's square for building, a pointy top for spinning! She thinks about all the shapes around her, and all sorts of shapes start to swirl around in her head . . .

hello circle!

Hello Kitty loves circles, especially when they are round balls and circus hoops!

hello square!

Hello Kitty loves squares, especially when she paints pretty pictures on them!

hello triangle!

Hello Kitty loves triangles, especially when they are yummy slices of pizza to share with friends!

hello oval!

**Hello Kitty loves ovals, especially the sparkly
ones that her ice skates make!**

hello rectangle!

Hello Kitty loves rectangles, especially when they are mirrors!

hello diamond!

Hello Kitty loves diamonds, especially when she hits a home run! Go, Hello Kitty, go!

hello star!

Hello Kitty loves stars, especially when they
twinkle! Let's make a wish!

hello heart!

Hello Kitty loves hearts, especially the big valentine that she made just for you!

hello crescent!

Hello Kitty loves crescents, especially the moon
up above in the twinkling night sky!

hello shapes!

Hello Kitty loves all the shapes around her! Can you name all the shapes in her room? How many circles, squares, triangles, ovals, rectangles, diamonds, stars, and hearts do you see?

Illustrated by Higashi Glaser

The Library of Congress has cataloged the original edition of this book as follows:

Glaser, Higashi.
Hello Kitty, hello shapes! : includes a punch-out stencil of shapes and fun project ideas! / Higashi Glaser.
p. cm.
Summary: Hello Kitty loves the many different shapes that she encounters in her everyday life. Includes ideas for shape-related projects.
ISBN 0-8109-4229-1
[1. Shape—Fiction. 2. Cats—Fiction.] I. Title.

PZ7.G48046 Hd 2003
[E]—dc21

2002014069

ISBN of this edition: 978-0-8109-8366-3

115 West 18th Street
New York, NY 10011
www.abramsbooks.com